MAGIC
PETS

Two books in one!

HOLLY WEBB

Scholastic Children's Books
An imprint of Scholastic Ltd
Euston House, 24 Eversholt Street, London, NW1 1DB, UK
Registered office: Westfield Road, Southam, Warwickshire, CV47 0RA
SCHOLASTIC and associated logos are trademarks and/or
registered trademarks of Scholastic Inc.

First published in the UK as *Magic Molly: The Witch's Kitten*
and *Magic Molly: The Wish Puppy* by Scholastic Ltd, 2009
This edition published by Scholastic Ltd, 2020

Text copyright © Holly Webb, 2009
Illustrations copyright © Erica Jane Waters, 2009

The rights of Holly Webb and Erica Jane Waters to be identified
as the author and illustrator of this work have been asserted by them.

ISBN 978 0702 30478 1

A CIP catalogue record for this book
is available from the British Library.
Printed by CPI Group (UK) Ltd, Croydon, CR0 4YY
Papers used by Scholastic Children's Books are made
from wood grown in sustainable forests.

1 3 5 7 9 10 8 6 4 2
www.scholastic.co.uk

www.holly-webb.com

MAGIC
PETS

THE WITCH'S KITTEN

For Alice, with love

Chapter One

Molly and Sparkle

Molly dashed across the yard, her school bag thudding against her side. "I'm just going to see Dad!"

"Don't be long, Molly! You need to change out of your school uniform!" Mum called.

"I'll just be a minute! I only want to see if anyone I know is in the waiting room," Molly promised, as she reached the surgery door.

"Me too! Me too!" her little sister

Kitty begged, but Mum took her into the house for juice instead.

Molly Smith was seven years old. She lived with her mum and dad and Kitty at Larkfield Farm, just on the edge of the town. It was a lovely place to live, with a huge field behind the house to play in, and, best of all, it was right across the farmyard from the vet's surgery!

Molly's mum and dad ran Larkfield Vets. Her dad, Sam, was the vet and her mum, Jo, was one of the veterinary nurses, but she only worked part-time now.

Molly pushed the door open. Her heart gave an excited little thump. This was her favourite moment of the day. She looked eagerly round as the door swung closed behind her. Larkfield Farm Vets was usually really busy, and Molly always felt like she was missing the most interesting animals while she was at school! Today the waiting room was quiet, with only a grumpy-looking dog, and one lady with a cat-basket.

Molly knew the lady – it was Sarah, who worked at the flower shop just down the road from the farm. Molly and Kitty and their mum would walk past her cottage when they were out exploring, and Sarah sometimes invited them in for a biscuit. Molly liked to go, because Sarah had three gorgeous cats, and they all loved Molly to stroke them – even though Sarah said they were normally shy. Molly adored cats. And dogs. And mice and gerbils and parrots – well, anything with fur or feathers, really. . .

"Hi Sarah!" Molly knelt down a little way from the basket to peer in. "Who've you brought today?" Then she looked up excitedly. "Hey, that's not Mickey! Or Freckles or Maisy. Have you got *another* cat?"

Sarah nodded and sighed. "Yes. This is Sparkle. I suppose he's mine. . ."

Molly sat up and looked at her. "You suppose he is?" She frowned. "I don't understand."

"Sparkle just turned up in my garden a couple of days ago. I saw him on my way home from work, and said hello to him. I just thought he must belong to one of the neighbours. Then he nipped in while I was letting Freckles out – you know how she hates using the cat flap."

Molly giggled. Freckles was a *very* fussy

cat. She hated coming to the vets too.

"Anyway, he had his nose in one of our cat food bowls before I'd even shut the door. He was starving, poor kitten. Now it looks like he's adopted me."

"He's gorgeous," Molly said admiringly, peeking back into the basket. "Is he all grey?"

"Not even a white hair," Sarah agreed. "Oh, he's a real beauty." She shook her head, and sighed again, even while she was smiling down at the grey kitten.

Molly didn't notice the sigh. She was too busy looking at Sparkle. It was a little hard to see him properly in the depths of the basket, but she could tell he was beautiful, and so tiny. He had big, round, sparkling green eyes, and soft silver-grey fur. His whiskers were long, shiny and black.

Molly gazed delightedly down at him. How could such a lovely little kitten be a stray? His real owner must be very upset. Molly shuddered at the thought. If he were hers and she'd lost him, she wouldn't know *what* to do.

Sparkle looked up at Molly hopefully, and opened his mouth, showing a bright pink tongue. He gave a sad little mew that Molly knew meant, "Please take me out of this horrible basket!"

Molly smiled. "It won't be much

longer," she promised him. "My dad will see you in a minute."

Just then, Molly's dad popped his head round the door of the consulting room, and grinned at her. "I heard that. I wondered when you'd arrive, Molly. You're right though, I've finished with Mr Davies and Alf, so Sarah can come on in."

He held the door open for a man carrying a tank with a large lizard in it. Molly stared curiously as he carried it past her, wondering what was wrong with Alf. He looked bored, but that was all she

DR SAM SMITH.

could see, and she had a feeling lizards looked like that a lot of the time.

"Definitely try him on crickets," Molly's dad called after Mr Davies, and Molly shuddered. *Uuurgh*. She was desperate to have a pet of her own, but she definitely didn't want anything she had to feed on live creepy-crawlies.

Sarah picked up Sparkle's basket, and Molly hopefully sneaked into the consulting room behind her. She'd told Mum she'd be back in a minute, but she really wouldn't be very long, and she *was* a friend of Sarah's. . .

"I can see you lurking, Molly," her dad said, chuckling.

Sarah smiled down at her. "I don't mind Molly staying. She's so good with the cats anyway. Last time I brought Freckles here, she was hanging on to the basket with every claw until Molly coaxed her out."

"So, who do we have here?" Sam asked, trying to look inside the basket. Sparkle had hunched himself up at the back, knowing that something was about to happen.

"It's a new kitten, Dad!" Molly told him excitedly.

"Oh, so that's why you were so keen to stay! Wow, another one, Sarah?"

Sarah shook her head. "Yes and no. I was telling Molly, he's a stray." She opened the basket, and reached in, pulling out a scrabbling Sparkle. "Hey, hey, it's all right, little one."

Molly and her dad gazed at him, almost in a trance. He was so handsome!

"I would love to keep him – but Freckle is threatening to leave home, and Maisy and Mickey keep hiding in the

kitchen cupboards." Sarah sighed sadly.

"They don't want a new kitten in their house?" Molly asked, not really surprised.

"It isn't just that. Sparkle looks sweet, but he's a bit of a nightmare. He just seems – well, odd, I suppose." Sarah looked down at Sparkle, who was now sitting on the examining table, chewing on Sam's sleeve. "He doesn't seem to like sitting still, and he's the most accident-prone cat I've ever met! He's broken two vases, and the glass in the back door. And we've only had him three days!"

Molly and her dad gave Sparkle a surprised look. That was a lot of mess for one very small kitten.

"And he's shredded half the accounts for the flower shop. I don't even know how he did it, it was in tiny little bits all over the kitchen floor. I don't know, he just seems to have to *look* at something, and it breaks. . ." She looked hopefully at Molly's dad. "I don't suppose you know anyone who wants a kitten, do you?"

"A kitten *and* a built-in paper shredder? Hmm. I'll ask around." He tickled Sparkle under the chin. "He doesn't look troublesome. Is there anything you're worried about, or do you just want him checked over?"

There was a knock on the door just then, and one of the veterinary nurses popped her head round. "Molly, your mum just called me – were you supposed to be on your way home, by any chance?" She was grinning. It was a message she had to pass on most days!

Molly gave Sparkle a longing look, and sighed. "Sorry, Jenny, I'll come now. I totally forgot. I told Mum I was only popping in to say hello. See you later, Dad! Bye Sarah, bye Sparkle."

Sparkle gazed after her as she dashed to the door, and mewed again, sadly.

Sarah smiled. "Animals just love Molly, don't they?" she said to Molly's dad.

Sam Smith nodded. "I know. I wouldn't be surprised if she became a vet when she's older. Molly would be a fantastic vet. She's got a magic touch."

Sparkle was still staring at the slowly closing door, but as Sam said that he turned to look thoughtfully up at him. It was almost as if he thought so too. . .

Chapter Two

Sparkle's Secret

Molly thought about Sparkle lots that week. She really wanted to know how he was getting on at Sarah's and whether the other cats were starting to like him. Her dad had put up a notice in the surgery, telling people that Sparkle had been found, and did anyone know who he belonged to. Sarah had said she was going to put up some more round the town too.

"He didn't have a collar on, though,"

Molly's dad explained at breakfast on Friday. "I've a feeling we'll need to find a new home for him, if Sarah can't keep him."

Molly drifted into a daydream, imagining Sparkle's new home – with her. Sparkle sleeping curled up on her bed. Sparkle waiting to play with her when she came home from school. Sparkle sitting on her desk while she did her homework.

"No, Molly." Her mum's voice was firm, and Molly stared at her.

"What?" she asked, trying to look as though she hadn't been thinking about kittens at all.

"No, you are not having a cat. You're not old enough for your own pet yet. Your dad and I have seen too many animals who don't get properly looked after. You just need to be a bit older, that's all." Her mum smiled sympathetically. "Kitty's still very young for a pet, too. She'd be dressing a kitten in her doll's clothes!"

"And even if you were both old enough, from what Sarah said, I don't think I want that kitten in the house." Molly's dad shuddered.

Molly stared down at her toast, her eyes suddenly filling with tears. Poor little Sparkle. What if nobody wanted him?

Molly's grandad picked her up from school that afternoon with Kitty. He quite often did, when he wasn't working. He was the local blacksmith, and Molly loved

to help him by holding the horses and
ponies as he fitted their shoes.

"Grandad, can we walk home along the
lane?" Molly asked hopefully. "It's a really
nice day, and it hasn't rained for ages so it
won't be muddy."

Kitty jumped up and down, swinging from Grandad's hand. "Yes, yes! We can look for rabbits!" Kitty and Molly had once seen wild rabbits when they were walking down the lane in the early evening, and now Kitty watched for them every time.

"Sounds good to me. Here, Molly, give me that painting, you can't carry all of that." Molly had lots of bits that she'd gathered at school during the week, and she gratefully handed her painting over.

"That's a lovely cat, Molly. Is he one you saw at the surgery?" Grandad held the painting out to admire. Molly had drawn Sparkle as she remembered him, sitting on the surgery table, watching her sadly as she had to run back to the house.

She couldn't get his little face out of her mind somehow, which was odd, as she saw so many gorgeous pets at the surgery. Sparkle just seemed extra-special. She could imagine how he was feeling, back at Sarah's cottage, trying to fit in with the other cats, lonely and wishing for a home where someone really wanted him. . . It was almost as though she could hear him asking her to help.

"Yes, that's Sparkle. He's living with Sarah. We might see him if we go home past her cottage," Molly explained hopefully.

"I might have known it would be something to do with an animal," Grandad said, grinning. "Come on then. Cats and rabbits, let's see what we can find."

Molly and Kitty raced ahead as they came near to Sarah's cottage. They hadn't seen any rabbits by the little wood, but

Grandad had promised to take Kitty out on a special rabbit-watching trip one day soon, just before bedtime.

"I can see him!" Molly called back eagerly, her school bag bumping against her legs as she skidded to a halt. "Careful, Kitty, we might scare him if we run up too fast."

"Where is he? I want to see!" Kitty pulled against Molly's arm.

"Ssshhh, ssshhh, over there, look, on the fence." Molly pointed.

Sparkle was sitting on Sarah's front fence, perfectly posed on one of the fence posts, with his tail wrapped round his paws. He was staring interestedly up the lane towards them, his ears pricked forward, and his back a little stiff, in that way that cats look when they've just seen something important – like a mouse, or a butterfly to chase.

As Molly and
Kitty walked slowly
closer, Sparkle came
to meet them,
walking along the
top of the fence
like a tightrope
walker. He ducked
his head for them
to stroke his ears,

and purred loudly. Molly could feel how
glad he was to see her.

"I wanted to see you too," she whispered
happily, watching as Kitty gently tickled
Sparkle under his chin.

Then all of a sudden Sparkle tensed
up, pulling away from Kitty, and Molly
realized that Sarah's big black-and-white
cat Mickey had just popped through the

cat flap – Mickey was so big that he had to push himself through the hole and he really did seem to pop out. Mickey stopped short as soon as he saw Sparkle, and then he hissed, and the two cats glared at each other.

"What are they doing, Molly?" Kitty asked nervously.

"I don't think Mickey likes Sparkle very much," Molly explained. "Because Sparkle's living in his house, I suppose." Hopefully Molly leaned over the fence to try and distract the big tomcat. "Mickey! Puss-puss-puss! Come and see me!"

But for once Mickey ignored her. He stalked furiously across the garden and stopped by the fence, hissing loudly at Sparkle, his tail flicking back and forth.

Sparkle hissed back, but he was standing nervously on the fence now.

Mickey prowled backwards and forwards underneath him, his tail fluffing up to twice its normal size.

"Maybe we should tell Sarah," Molly muttered worriedly. "I don't want them to fight!"

But just then Sparkle gave up. He scooted along the fence and dashed up into the safety of the big apple tree. From up there he felt brave enough to hiss and spit back at Mickey.

Molly couldn't help giggling. Now she wasn't worried about the cats hurting each other, it was quite funny watching them – she could almost imagine the rude names Sparkle was shouting at Mickey!

Sarah came round the side of the cottage carrying a basket of gardening things. "Stop it, you two!" Sarah said crossly. "Oh, hello girls, hello Ted."

"We were just about to come and tell you," Molly said. "We weren't sure if they were going to have a fight."

Mickey gave Sparkle one last furious look and stomped grumpily back over to the cat flap, squeezing himself back in. Sparkle sat on his branch, grumbling to himself, and licking his paws indignantly. He clearly wasn't at all grateful to Sarah for interrupting.

"To be honest, Molly," Sarah sighed, "I don't know what to do with them. I'm beginning to think I'm going to have to take Sparkle to the animal shelter. Him being here just isn't working. But it's so sad — he'll hate it there, shut in a tiny run. He's such a stubborn little cat, and he likes his own way."

"No one else wants him?" Molly asked miserably. Oh, if only Mum and Dad would let her have Sparkle!

Sarah shook her head. "No one that I can find."

Sparkle finished licking his paws, and

gave himself a little shake. Clearly he felt back to normal now. He stood up, and picked his way delicately along the branch to Molly. He gazed down at her, his huge green eyes glinting with excitement.

Molly laughed, rather sadly. "I can see why you call him Sparkle," she told Sarah. "His eyes really do."

Sarah seemed surprised. She looked down at Sparkle, with an odd expression on her face. "Do you know, Molly, I hadn't even thought about it before. . ." She frowned to herself. "I didn't name him Sparkle. I'm sure I didn't. It was just – his name. But he hadn't a collar, so how did I know?"

Sparkle jumped down on to the fence, and trotted back to Molly and Kitty. He stretched out his head to Molly, offering her his ears to scratch. She rubbed his soft, silky fur, and he let out a deep, rumbling purr of delight. Then he half stood on his hind paws, obviously wanting her to pick him up for a cuddle.

Molly let him jump into her arms, amazed at how light he was. She held him against her shoulder, his green eyes gazing into her blue ones, and wished and wished he was hers.

It was as though a river rushed through her mind all at once. Glittering images seemed to burst in on her, and such feelings! New things and loneliness and a desperate wish to go home. She saw huge trees, and an old lady who had lots of delicious food, and butterflies that were such fun to chase. . . *Please take me home!*

Molly jumped, dropping Sparkle, who sprang out of her arms, and leaped back to the fence. Molly stared at him in amazement, cradling her hand, and he stared back.

If cats could smile, Sparkle was smiling now. A loving, anxious, hopeful smile that was so clearly asking her for something. Had he *really* just spoken to her? She was sure he had asked her to take him home. It was strange, and a little scary, but Molly still couldn't help bubbling with wonder and happiness. She'd always dreamed of being able to talk to the animals she loved so much. Was it actually happening? Or had she just imagined it?

"Oh, Molly, I'm so sorry, did he bite you?" Sarah asked anxiously, looking at her hand.

"N-no." Molly murmured. She couldn't say what had happened. She didn't *know*. And if she said that Sparkle had *talked* to her, and that he'd felt as if he were made of glitter, and gold, and shining light, they would all think she was being silly.

Instead she just stared at the little grey cat, wondering what he'd done to her — and what he *was*.

And what she was supposed to do about it.

Chapter Three

A Midnight Visitor

Molly was silent all the way home. It was half because she couldn't believe what had just happened, and half because she was so upset that Sparkle might have to go to an animal shelter. It was lucky that Grandad explained to Mum, because Molly couldn't have told her about it without crying. If only they could find his real owner! Sarah loved cats, and if even she couldn't face keeping him, he'd never have a home. He might be at the animal shelter for ever.

He wants to go home, Molly thought miserably. *I know cats can't talk, but I'm sure he asked me to take him home!* Molly had never felt anything like the pictures and thoughts that had rushed through her when she was holding the little grey kitten. Strangely enough, that amazing stream of thoughts had felt almost *sparkly*.

Maybe that's what he was named for, Molly wondered, gazing at her fish fingers without really seeing them. *Not his sparkling green eyes at all*. Then she remembered what Sarah had said about Sparkle's name. That was *really* weird. How could a cat tell someone their name? And how had she known what Sparkle wanted, if he hadn't told her?

It sounded almost like magic. . .

Molly was dreaming about having her own kitten – a green-eyed grey kitten who looked just like Sparkle. He was curled up on her lap, purring deeply as she stroked him. Molly smiled in her sleep, her fingers twitching. Then her dream-kitten stood up on her lap, his ears pricked, and mewed excitedly. He turned and put his paws up on her chest, padding at her with his paws, mewing again, trying to tell her something.

Molly rolled over in bed, muttering worriedly to herself. Then she sat up suddenly. This wasn't a dream. That really was mewing! Sad, weary mewing from outside her bedroom window.

Molly blinked, and pinched herself to check that this wasn't just a very odd dream. Ow! No, she was definitely

awake. The night-light from the landing
was shining into her room, but it was
still half-dark, the room full of scary
shadows. It must be the middle of the
night.

*Why would I dream about a black kitten,
and then hear one mewing outside my
window?* Molly thought to herself. It had
to be Sparkle, it just had to. He had been
sending her a dream-message! Still, it was
difficult to make herself get out of bed. It
was so dark!

She pushed back her duvet and walked slowly over to the window, her heart thudding hard with excitement and fear. She grabbed her bedroom curtains, and took a deep breath, then pulled them open quickly.

Even though she'd been almost sure that Sparkle would be there, she still jumped back when he pressed his nose against the dark window and meowed loudly. Sparkle stood up with his front paws on the window, scrabbling against the glass. "Let me in! Oh, please let me in!"

Molly just stared at him. It was obvious that that was what he meant, but he'd actually said it. Hadn't he? A cat really had spoken to her. . . Molly put her hand over her mouth to stop herself from laughing out loud in pure delight. She didn't want to explain this to her sleepy, and probably grumpy mum and dad!

Sparkle batted the window again. "It's so cold out here! Open the window, Molly, please!"

Molly unfastened the window catch — the old farmhouse had pretty, diamond-patterned windows with deep windowsills — and waved to Sparkle to scoot along so she could open the window. He hunched himself up against the wall, and then squidged himself through the window as soon as Molly creaked it open.

"It's freezing out there," Sparkle squeaked as he leaped down from the windowsill. "You sleep very soundly, don't you? I was mewing for ages, you know." He gazed up at her, his ears laid a little back. He was obviously frozen.

"Sorry," Molly whispered, staring at him as he made himself comfortable on her bed. He had fluffed up all his fur to keep himself warm, and he looked like her nana's old-fashioned powder puff.

"Come on," Sparkle said, making himself a little nest in her duvet. "Won't you cuddle me while we work out a plan? You're lovely and warm."

"A plan?" Molly repeated, as she obediently got back into bed. She pulled the duvet up round her, and sat hugging her knees and watching this strange little creature who seemed to have taken over her bedroom.

Sparkle
looked up
at her, his
huge green
eyes full of
surprise. "Well,
of course! You
are going to take me

home, aren't you?" He stared hopefully
at her, his eyes round and worried. "Oh,
please, you have to!"

Molly gaped at him. She didn't know
what to say. Then she took a deep breath.
"I do?" she asked politely.

"You're the only person who's heard
me talking, so far," Sparkle explained.
He sounded rather upset. "I've asked
everybody," he added miserably. "No one
listened."

Molly leaned forward, interested. "Nobody else can understand you?" she asked curiously. "Only me?"

"I thought Sarah *might*," Sparkle said thoughtfully. "It was as though she almost did, but then she seemed not to want to."

"Maybe it's because she's a grown-up," Molly wondered.

"Probably." Sparkle nodded. "Yes, that might be it. She's too old to believe."

"And . . . I can hear you because I believe?" Molly asked shyly.

Sparkle gave her a cat-smile, crinkling up his eyes. "I think you must be quite special. Like my owner. That's why you're the only one who can take me back to her."

Molly nodded excitedly. "Of course I will. Where does she live?"

Sparkle sighed sadly. "I don't know!" He

was obviously embarrassed. He hunched up his shoulders, and then started to lick his paw very quickly so as not to have to look at Molly. "If I knew — I could — go back — by myself, couldn't I?" he said, his voice rather muffled by the paw-licking.

"Oh. . ." Molly said doubtfully. "But . . . I don't know where you live, either. . . Don't you have *any* idea? Is it far away?"

"Oh no, not very." Sparkle sat up eagerly. He climbed up the duvet towards Molly and started to explain. "You see, I was exploring. I *am* allowed, you know. But I'm not supposed to go out of the clearing. . ." He sighed, and his whiskers drooped.

"But you did?" Molly asked gently, stroking behind his ears.

Sparkle purred, twisting his head against her fingers. "Yes," he admitted. "Not very

far, though. I was chasing a butterfly.
The biggest one I've ever seen!" His eyes
sparkled brightly. "I almost caught it, too.
Then it fluttered off between the trees,
and I'd so nearly got it, I thought it
wouldn't matter. I only
followed it a *little*
way, really." His
voice was sad
suddenly, and
he pulled
himself away
and turned
his back on
Molly, sitting very still. He muttered the
rest. "Then it disappeared, which wasn't
fair, and when I looked round to go back,
I couldn't quite see which trees I was
meant to go past. That butterfly cheated."
Molly couldn't help smiling. He sounded

just like Kitty. It made her see how young Sparkle was — even though he could talk, he was still only a very little cat.

"Don't worry, Sparkle. I'll get you home, I know you live by trees now," she told him encouragingly. "Are there any other clues you can tell me? What does your owner's house look like? Oh, and what's her name? I might know her, I know lots of people in Larkhill, because so many of them come to our vet's surgery."

Sparkle turned round and looked at her hopefully, but then he shook his head. "I don't think you'll know her. She doesn't often come into the town. She likes to be quiet and peaceful, and she says people are too noisy. But she doesn't mind me," he said proudly. "She's teaching me lots of things. Only I forgot about not going too far, and that's the most important thing of all." He sighed. "I probably won't get a chocolate mouse after tea."

"What about her house, then?" Molly asked, grinning to herself. He was so sweet!

Sparkle blinked. He was obviously still thinking about chocolate mice. "It's a small house. But it's lovely and cosy. My owner calls it a cottage," he said thoughtfully. "And there are lots of trees, like I said before. . . Oh, and there's a stream! I went across that after the butterfly."

Molly stared at him. She had a horrible feeling all of a sudden. "Sparkle, did you go past a big tree, one that had fallen over and had moss and toadstools growing all over it?"

"Oh yes!" Sparkle agreed happily. "I forgot! Well done, Molly! You know where my home is, don't you? Can you take me back? Please?"

Molly stared at him silently, her eyes wide with panic. He was so little, and he was trusting her to take him home. And the awful thing was, she *did* know where he meant.

In the clearing, past the old hollow tree, across the stream, deep in the middle of Larkhill Wood.

Where the witch lived. . .

Chapter Four

The Magic Glitter

Of course, she should have known. *Who else but a witch would have a kitten who talked*, Molly thought to herself, as she watched Sparkle sleeping, stretched out on her pillow. He was snoozing blissfully,

his paws curling and uncurling as he dreamed – probably he was thinking of chocolate mice again, or scampering after those butterflies. He was so sure Molly could take him home. She couldn't let him down. But it was Larkfield Wood!

Everyone in the town knew that the middle of the wood was special, and secret, and haunted. Everyone at school said so. None of Molly's friends had ever been to the middle of the wood.

Last summer she and two of her friends from school, Kieran and Lucy, had gone on a picnic with Lucy's mum and dad to Larkfield Wood, and they'd played hide-and-seek. Kieran had dared them to run up and touch the old hollow tree, and Molly had just about managed it. She'd brushed it with her fingertips and raced away, feeling sick with fear, and sure that something horrible was chasing her.

Lucy hadn't even touched the tree.

She'd said she didn't care if Kieran told everyone in their class she was a big fat baby, *she wasn't going near that tree for anyone*. And when they went back to their picnic spot, and told Lucy's parents what they'd been playing, Lucy's mum had shaken her head, and shuddered.

"I don't blame you, Lucy!" she said, giving her a big hug. "I wouldn't either. This part of the wood is lovely, but no one goes too far in. Never past the old hollow tree."

"Why?" demanded Kieran. His mum and dad hadn't lived in Larkfield all that long, and so he didn't know all the stories.

"It's where the witch lives," Lucy's mum said simply. And she sounded so certain that even Kieran didn't laugh. He just looked thoughtfully back through the trees. Molly had stared down at her fingers, and then rubbed them hard on her shorts. They'd felt sticky, and dirty, even though they looked clean.

Now Sparkle wanted her to go even further into the wood, and over the stream. He needed Molly to find a witch's cottage – and a witch!

I suppose I could just leave him by the hollow tree, Molly thought. *But then he might not be able to find his way, and he could be lost in the scary wood, all alone. I'd have to see him all the way home, I'd have to. . .*

Molly lay awake long into the night. She couldn't let Sparkle be taken off to an animal shelter, he would hate it so much, but no one else wanted him. And anyway, Sparkle didn't want a new owner, he wanted to go home.

It wasn't just going all the way into the wood that was the only problem, Molly thought, wriggling round in bed for the thousandth time. How was she going to get Mum to let her disappear off to the woods on a secret journey? It was Saturday tomorrow, so at least she didn't have school, but she wasn't allowed out by herself except in their garden and the field. Mum would never let her go to the woods on her own.

Molly sighed, and tucked a fold of the duvet over Sparkle, in case Mum or Kitty came in early in the morning and spotted him.

When she fell asleep at last, Molly kept dreaming about enormous trees that walked, and tapped her shoulders with their long, scratchy branches. It was horrible, and she was very glad to wake up, and see the sunshine pouring through the curtains she'd left open last night. Somehow the thought of the wood wasn't quite so scary in the daylight. But there was still Mum and Dad to worry about.

Molly stared down at Sparkle, and as she watched, he opened one green eye and stared back. Then he yawned hugely, showing his tiny pointy white teeth.

"Hello," he said sleepily. Then he sat up and peered into her eyes. "What's the matter?" he asked, his ears laying back against his head. "You look worried."

Molly sighed. "I'm so sorry, Sparkle, but I don't know how I'm going to manage to take you back home. I can't exactly tell my mum I'm going off to the woods because a kitten told me to, can I?"

Sparkle nodded, and licked a paw, in a considering sort of way. "Can't you just tell her you're going for a walk?"

Molly shook her head. "No. They wouldn't let me go on my own."

Sparkle nodded. "Oh. No, I see. Like I'm not supposed to." He stared sadly at the pattern on the duvet. Suddenly he sat up straight, looking excited. "I know! We'll do a spell."

"Can you do spells?" Molly asked doubtfully.

"Oh yes! I've done lots. Well, some. If

you help, I'm sure we can do it. Do you
have anything glittery?"

Molly looked round her room. "Like a
necklace?"

"No, no, no! I need magic dust, and I
shouldn't think you have any of that, so
we have to make some." Sparkle leaped
off the bed, and started to prowl around
the room, sniffing hopefully.

Molly climbed out of bed and followed
him. "Look, what about this?" She showed
him the special art set that her nana
had sent her, which had six different
colours of glitter in little tubes. It was her
favourite thing.

"Perfect!" Sparkle's whiskers twitched delightedly as Molly held the open tube of pink glitter under his nose. "But not so close, or I'll sneeze," he added practically.

"What will happen when we use the magic dust?" Molly asked breathlessly, her heart thumping with excitement.

Sparkle looked as though he hadn't planned that far. "Um. I'm not sure." He wrinkled his nose thoughtfully. "What do we *want* to happen?"

Molly wrinkled her nose as well. "Well . . . I suppose we want my mum and dad to let us go to Larkfield Wood. But − it's not that I don't think the magic will work, Sparkle − it's just that I'm still not sure Mum will let me go off to the woods. She'd say no to that even if she was *covered* in magic glitter, I bet she would."

They looked at each worriedly. Then Molly gave an excited squeak. "I know! Let's ask Mum and Dad if we can *all* go on a picnic to Larkfield Wood. And the magic can persuade them to say yes! Then perhaps we can find your home while we're all in the wood."

"Yes!" Sparkle ran round Molly in circles, so fast his fur went blurry. "That's just right." He skidded to a stop and jumped back on to Molly's bed. "Come on, bring the glitter. We've got to turn it into magic dust." He stared at the tube of glitter in Molly's hand, his little grey forehead wrinkling as he thought. "You need to think about your parents for me, Molly – this magic dust is for them, you see. And now we blow on it! Come on!"

He blew a slow, careful breath on to the tube of glitter, and Molly blew too,

very softly and gently. She was trying to
hold a picture of her mum and dad in
her mind at the same time, and it was
tricky. But to her amazement the glitter
swirled up and out of the tube, spiralling
round and round, sparkling and twinkling.

It whirled round Molly, wrapping her in a shimmery pink cocoon that smelled like strawberries, before it all whooshed back into its little tube again. The fiddly little stopper flew back into the tube with a pop.

Molly giggled. "That was magic! I can't believe we just did magic in my bedroom!"

Sparkle purred proudly. "I *am* clever," he admitted, ducking his head as though he was a little bit shy. "Now all we have to do is sprinkle the glitter around your parents, and Kitty." Sparkle nodded to himself, clearly pleased with their work. "Now can I have some breakfast, please? Doing magic makes me very hungry."

Molly crept downstairs and found him some tuna fish that her mum had left in the fridge from making her a packed lunch the other day. Sparkle sniffed it doubtfully, but then wolfed it down. "Is there any more?" he asked hopefully.

Molly shook her head. "No, and we haven't got any cat food. Sssshh! I can hear someone. Hide!" She looked round in a panic for somewhere to hide a little grey kitten, but Sparkle just gave her a mischievous look, and vanished.

Molly gasped with shock, then giggled as she realized what he'd done. He was so clever – and so naughty!

"I'll be back soon!" A whispery little voice seemed to float on the air. "After you've all had breakfast, use the magic glitter, and we'll be off!"

Chapter Five

Larkfield Wood

It was a beautiful day. Even though it was late September, the sun was warm, and the trees were just starting to show yellow and orange leaves amongst the green. The spell was working beautifully. They were very close to the old hollow tree. Molly tried hard to feel more pleased. . .

"This was a very good idea, Molly," Mum said, starting to unpack their picnic. "A lovely way to spend a Saturday."

Molly smiled. She looked over her

shoulder, peering into her backpack. Mum and Dad thought it was full of her rain jacket and a sun hat – Mum liked to be prepared, whatever the weather. She had just about got the sun hat in, but peeping out from underneath it was Sparkle. She could see his green eyes glittering with excitement.

"We're close!" he whispered. "I can feel it, Molly! I'm nearly home!"

Kitty was jumping about cheerfully. "Let's go and explore!" she cried. "Can we look for rabbits? I bet rabbits live here!"

"Let's have lunch first," Dad said. "I need a rest after that long walk. Come and sit down, girls."

Molly looked doubtfully at her backpack. She wasn't sure Sparkle could manage to stay still for much longer. The backpack had already done a lot of wriggling while they were walking. She sat down, making sure it was behind her, and none of the others could see it.

"Ham sandwich, Molly?" Mum held one out.

"Ahem!" A kitten cough sounded behind her, and Molly grinned. She broke off a big corner, and carefully dropped it by the backpack, while she pretended to look for her sunglasses.

Sparkle had two sandwiches and a sausage roll, and he argued for Molly's chocolate biscuit too, but Molly was sure biscuits weren't good for cats.

"Goodness, Molly, you are hungry today!" Mum commented. "It must have been the long walk."

Molly nodded, trying not to smile. While Mum and Dad packed away the rubbish, she peeped round at her backpack. Sparkle was awfully quiet.

Sparkle had gone!

Molly gasped, and grabbed the bag, hoping that she was just being stupid and he was there after all.

"Are you all right, Molly?" Dad asked, looking up.

"Oh! Yes, I . . . I just sat on a stone, that's all." Molly gave him a half-smile. Sparkle couldn't have just left, not without saying goodbye. And besides, he hadn't been sure where in the wood his home was. She gazed at the trees through tear-filled eyes. She couldn't believe he'd gone.

"Prrrp!" A little purring noise made her jump.

Sparkle popped his head out from behind a clump of ferns and grinned at her. "Come on!" he whispered. "Let's go and find the cottage!"

Molly was so relieved. She jumped up, almost forgetting she was on a secret mission. Then she remembered. "Mum, can I go and explore?"

Her mum looked unsure. Molly stared at her hopefully, and felt in her jeans pocket for the magic dust – they'd brought the last few sprinkles from the bottom of the tube, just in case.

"It'll be all right, if Molly's careful not to go too far," Dad said helpfully. "Make sure you stay where you can hear us if we call, won't you?"

"Oh yes!" Molly agreed, already following a little grey tail that was skipping off through the trees.

"Don't go disturbing any witches!" Dad shouted after her, laughing.

"I won't!" Molly called back, wishing over and over that that wasn't exactly what she was planning to do.

A couple of minutes later, Molly looked over her shoulder nervously. She could only just see Dad's red sweatshirt now.

She knew they weren't far at all from their picnic spot, but it felt like she and Sparkle were on their own in the wood. It was silent – just like her dream. The trees weren't actually following her, but they did have long twiggy branches, that looked as if they might reach out and catch her hair.

"What's the matter?" Sparkle asked, trotting back to her.

Molly gave up trying to pretend she wasn't scared. It wasn't working very well. "I don't like it here," she whispered. "It's spooky."

Sparkle looked around, surprised. "Is it?"

Molly rubbed her hands over her arms. She was cold, even in the warm sunlight. "Yes," she said firmly. "I know you don't think so, but it is! Oh, look, there's the hollow tree." Molly pointed, her hand

shaking slightly. She could just hear Kitty
laughing at something in the distance.
They aren't far! she told herself firmly.

"Oh yes! Well done, Molly!" Sparkle
ran ahead and leaped on to the tree,
running up and down it in a mad kitten
dance. "Is it much further from here?" he
asked her hopefully, when he eventually
stopped twirling around after his tail.

"I'm not sure," Molly said, taking a deep, shivery breath. "I think we just have to look. Do you remember where you were when you saw the hollow tree, on the day you got lost?"

Sparkle hopped down, and trotted over to the side of the clearing. "Maybe this way?" he said thoughtfully. "Or that way? Oooh, there are some gorgeous smells over here! It smells like mouse!" He bounded off behind a bush.

"Don't go too far!" Molly called anxiously. "Don't get lost. . ."

But then her voice trailed off.

There was someone else coming through the trees. . .

Chapter Six

Sparkle's Gift

Walking towards her was an old lady who looked quite like her nana. She was smiling, but she looked anxious. "You haven't seen a kitten, have you, while you were walking? A grey kitten, quite small. The silly little thing went off exploring, a few days ago." She sighed. "I'm sure he's safe, I'd know if he wasn't, but I do wish I knew where he'd got to."

Molly gulped, and said very quietly and very fast, "He's-over-there!" Then she shut

her mouth with a snap. She didn't think
it was a good idea to talk to witches. Not
without being asked, anyway.

The old lady looked at her closely. "What
did you say, dear? Are you all right?"

Molly nodded. She was still too nervous

to say anything, but the witch didn't seem as frightening as she had expected. She wasn't even wearing black.

Suddenly the old lady gasped. "Sparkle! Oh, you're back, you silly kitten, where have you been?" And she crouched down, reaching out to Sparkle, who was racing across the clearing towards them. He was so excited that he was leaving a trail of tiny pink and golden stars floating behind him as his paws touched the grass, and he flung himself into the old lady's arms, purring with delight.

Molly laughed, his happiness was so catching, but she couldn't help feeling the tiniest bit sad. She wouldn't see Sparkle again now. It had been so lovely to imagine him being hers, but now she knew it was never going to happen. She gave a little sigh, and realized that Sparkle was telling the old lady about his adventures.

"And Molly had some pink glitter, and I put a spell on it, so she could bring me home!" he finished triumphantly.

The witch looked a little bewildered, but she smiled gratefully at Molly. "Thank you so much, Molly dear. It was very brave of you to come, and very clever to think of bringing everyone on a picnic. I can't think that you wanted to come deeper into the wood, did you?"

Molly smiled shyly and shook her head.

"She was scared," Sparkle said. "*I* wasn't." He jumped down and started to bat at grass seeds with his tiny paws.

The witch gave Molly an apologetic look. "Kittens can be very rude sometimes," she said, smiling. "Won't you come and tell me how you found Sparkle? Let's sit on the old tree for a bit, my legs aren't what they used to be."

Molly looked at the tree. Somehow it didn't seem scary any more. It had dark green velvety moss that looked just like cushions. She sat down next to the old lady, and they watched Sparkle stalking an imaginary mouse.

"Can you speak to all animals?" the witch asked Molly curiously.

Molly stared back at her. "I don't think so," she said in surprise. "Sparkle is the only one who's ever spoken to *me*. Do you think I might meet more animals who talk?" she asked hopefully. She explained about living at the vet's.

The witch nodded slowly. "I think you've been given a very special gift. It must be for a reason."

Molly stared worriedly back at her. That sounded a bit scary. "You mean, I have to go on a – a quest, or something like that?" she asked, thinking about stories that she'd read.

"No, I think you should stay right where you are," the witch said, smiling. "Sparkle found you, didn't he, when he needed someone. You see so many animals, you'll just need to keep an eye out for the special ones. The ones who need your gift."

Molly nodded, smiling to herself. More magical animals! It was so exciting! Then she looked anxious. "But what if I can't help? I only managed to bring Sparkle home because I knew where you lived. And I almost didn't help, even then," she added very quietly, feeling rather ashamed of herself.

"But you *did*, Molly. That's what matters. It wouldn't have been brave if Sparkle had just lived down the street, would it?" The witch stared thoughtfully into the distance, and then reached a hand into the air. When she brought it down again, something glittery was dangling from it. She passed it to Molly, who was watching wide-eyed. "For you, to say thank you."

Sparkle ran back and jumped on to Molly's lap to see what it was. "Oh!

Pretty!" he said, patting at it with a paw. It was a silver chain with a little stone pendant dangling from it, in the shape of a cat's head.

"It's beautiful," Molly breathed, holding it in her hand.

"It opens, do you see?" the witch explained, pointing out a tiny catch at the side. She took a tiny pair of golden scissors from her pocket. "You can put something inside."

She beckoned to Sparkle, and whispered in his ear. He twitched his tail reluctantly. "*Must* I?" he whined. "If you cut one off, they won't match. Oh, I suppose so!" He pointed his nose towards her, sighing heavily, and she snipped off one of his whiskers.

"Now, put it inside the locket," the witch explained, dropping the shining whisker into Molly's hand. It sparkled a little as she folded it round into the tiny space. "If you ever need our help, you can call us with it, you see."

"It's very special, you know, one of my whiskers. Thank you, Molly, for bringing me home." Sparkle put his paws on Molly's arm, and reached up to touch her nose with his. A kitten kiss. Molly smiled down at him, feeling the glittery magic as his whiskers brushed her cheek.

Somewhere a bird called, breaking the spell, and Molly gasped. "Oh! What time is it?" she asked, jumping down from the tree. "We've been away ages, haven't we?" It felt as though she and Sparkle had been in that strange, magical wood for hours.

The witch smiled. "They won't have missed you. It's really only been a few minutes."

Molly nodded slowly. Had it only been that long? It felt as if her whole life had changed, in just a moment. She leaned over to hug Sparkle one last time, and he purred gratefully in her ear.

"Goodbye!" Molly called, and she ran on a few steps, anxious to get back, and see whether her parents really hadn't worried about her. She turned to wave one last time, to say thank you for her beautiful present.

But they were gone. There was no old lady sitting on the hollow tree, no sparkling grey cat.

Molly stared through the trees, a little doubtfully, and then her hand closed tightly around the cat locket. "Goodbye!" she whispered, smiling, sure they could hear her. Then she ran on into the clearing where she could see Kitty and her parents waving. Molly waved back excitedly.

She was already wondering what her next adventure would be.

MAGIC
PETS

THE WISH PUPPY

For Alice, with love

Chapter One

The Saddest Puppy

Molly lay in the long grass, staring up at the sky. It was a deep end-of-summer September blue, and cloudless. It seemed to be a day for sunbathing, or picnics, or an outing, but Molly wasn't in the mood.

She couldn't help feeling a teensy bit sad. A week ago she had said goodbye to Sparkle, the wonderful, magical, *naughty* little black kitten who'd turned her life upside down. Sparkle had been lost, and he'd found Molly and asked her to help him find his home again. That was when Molly had discovered she could talk to animals! She still had to pinch herself to believe it was true.

Molly missed having a cheeky talking kitten hiding out in her bedroom. She really wanted to meet another magical animal, now that she knew she had a special gift. But no magical creatures had turned up yet, and it was beginning to feel like it had all been a dream.

"Moll-eeee! Moll-eeee!" Her little sister

Kitty was standing on the orchard gate, calling to her. "Molly, where are you? I need you to *play* with me!"

Molly thought about just staying where she was. The grass was long, and there was a good chance Kitty couldn't see her. She didn't much want to play mermaids, Kitty's favourite game of the moment.

Then a thought struck her. *I wonder if there really are mermaids*, she said to herself, her eyes widening. *If there are actual witches, and kittens who can talk, maybe mermaids are real too! Oh, I wish we were going to the seaside soon!* Her nana lived by the sea, and Molly could imagine walking along the beach and finding a mermaid hiding in a rockpool, her hair like swirling seaweed.

Molly stood up, her head full of mermaids and sparkling sea, but Kitty had already run off to find someone else to join in her game.

"Molly!" It was her dad now, calling her from the vet's surgery on the other side of the old farmyard. He was looking out of the window at her. "Molly, do you want to come over? It's nearly the end

of morning surgery, I could do with a helper. Mrs Hunter's brought her new puppy to see me. I'm sure she'd love to show her off."

"What sort of dog is she?" Molly asked excitedly.

"She's a spaniel, a King Charles spaniel. Lovely dogs. Mrs Hunter needs some company, and small dogs like those don't need too much walking. She's just bringing

Star in because she's a new puppy. It's always good to get a new pet checked over."

Molly ran across the yard and pushed open the door to the surgery, bumping into Jenny, the veterinary nurse, as she was coming out.

"Hi Molly! Are you coming to visit your dad?"

Molly nodded. "He said I could see Mrs Hunter's new puppy," she told Jenny excitedly.

Jenny smiled. "The puppy looked quite shy – I think she needs your 'magic touch', Molly!"

Molly nodded happily and went in to the consulting room. "Hi Dad! Hi, Mrs Hunter!"

Mrs Hunter was an elderly lady that Molly had known for ages from her visits to the surgery. Molly had been really sad when Mrs Hunter's last dog, a Westie called Morris, had died earlier in the year. But her dad had pointed out that Morris was fourteen, which was a good age for a dog. Mrs Hunter had missed him loads, though, and it had taken her a while to decide she wanted another dog.

"Ohhh, she's gorgeous!" Molly breathed, as she caught sight of the little golden brown

and white dog. The puppy was peeping out over Mrs Hunter's arm, looking nervously round the surgery.

Mrs Hunter smiled, but she didn't look quite as happy as Molly thought someone with a beautiful new puppy should.

Molly's dad patted Star as Mrs Hunter put her on the examining table. The puppy was mostly a soft golden colour, with gorgeous, long brown ears, and a few pretty chestnut spots on her back. "She's beautiful! She came from somewhere round here, did you say?"

Mrs Hunter nodded. "Yes, I got her from a farm not far away. They breed dogs too, they have a lovely kennels in one of their barns." She stroked the little dog's head gently, but the look she gave her was anxious.

"And how's she settling in?" Molly's dad tickled the puppy under the chin, but she was crouched on the table looking scared.

Molly looked at her worriedly. There was something odd here. A lot of dogs

were scared to be at the vet's — her dad
was always very careful about which
animals Molly was allowed to touch, in
case a frightened creature bit her — but
this seemed different. Star looked so sad!

Mrs Hunter smiled. "Well — it's

different. I suppose I'm still missing
Morris a little. But Star is lovely. I'm sure
we'll soon settle down together."

Molly's dad nodded. "It just takes time.

She looks very loving." He went over to the shelves to get the equipment for Star's vaccinations, and the little dog watched him quietly. She didn't even flinch though, just hung her head, her whiskers brushing the table.

"Can I stroke her?" Molly asked, desperate to cheer the puppy up, and Mrs Hunter nodded. Molly gently ran her hand down Star's back, admiring her silky fur. But then she stood back, blinking. She could *feel* Star's sadness. The puppy was so unhappy! This wasn't just a young dog taking a while to settle in, something was wrong.

Very carefully, Molly lifted Star up and cuddled her. Most puppies would have wriggled and squirmed in excitement, but Star just lay limply in Molly's arms. Molly stroked her gently, and a wave of loneliness washed over her, a feeling that she'd lost someone very special. The sadness was so strong that Molly felt like crying and she almost dropped Star in surprise.

Star suddenly gave a little squeak and lifted her head, her huge brown eyes sparkling with hope. She put a paw on Molly's arm and gazed up at her. Molly's mind was suddenly filled with a joyful whisper.

"You can hear me!"

Chapter Two

Star's Story

Star wasn't ill, so after she'd had her vaccinations, Mrs Hunter picked her up to take her home. Molly really wanted to say something, to stop her, but how could she? Mrs Hunter and Dad wouldn't understand if she told them something was wrong. Star looked perfectly healthy.

Star had scrabbled a little as Mrs Hunter carried her out of the surgery, gazing over her owner's shoulder at Molly. Her eyes were pleading, and Molly was sure she could hear her still. *Please, please help me. . .*

Star kept popping into Molly's head all week. Especially those big, dark-brown puppy eyes. She had found another magical animal! Molly wanted to dance, she was so excited, but at the same time she couldn't help worrying what was wrong with Star. Molly was sure that she'd never *felt* anything so strong from a dog before. It was just like the magical energy that had rushed through her when she had first touched Sparkle, the kitten.

Molly had always been good at

understanding what animals wanted, but this had been different. Molly just wished she'd said something back, told Star she had understood.

I shouldn't have let her go! Molly thought to herself crossly. *Why did I? It was just such a shock, I didn't think. I really have to find Star, and help her. She asked me to!*

But Molly didn't even know where Mrs Hunter lived, or she'd have tried to get Mum to go that way for some reason. Larkfield wasn't a big town, she was sure she could have made something up! Now all she could do was look out for Mrs Hunter and Star while she was on her way to school, or out with Mum and Kitty.

As they were coming home from school on Wednesday, Molly spotted a lady in the High Street with a dog that looked just like Star. Funnily enough, it wasn't the dog's golden brown fur that made her so sure it was Star. Instead it was the sad way the dog's ears were drooping. Mrs Hunter was looking down at her worriedly as the little dog trailed along at the end of her pretty red lead.

Without even thinking, Molly chased after them. She was halfway down the street before Mum noticed she was gone, and called after her in horror. "Molly! Come back!"

Molly hesitated. She knew she had to go back, or Mum would be really cross, but it was Star! Just there! And she still looked so sad, and in need of Molly's help. Molly gave Mum an apologetic look and turned to keep running.

But it was too late. Mrs Hunter was already disappearing round the corner. Just as Star turned the corner of the street, she looked back, and Molly thought she saw a sudden flash of hope in the puppy's big dark eyes. But then she was gone, into the crowd.

Molly sighed, and walked slowly back to Mum and Kitty. Mum was furious with her for running off, and she hadn't even been able to help!

Then at lunch on Saturday, Molly's dad said, between bites of ham sandwich, that Star was back. Molly hadn't been able to

visit the surgery that morning – Mum
had taken her and Kitty clothes shopping
because it was turning cold and Molly
had grown a lot over the summer.

Molly choked on her juice. "What do
you mean, she's back?" she spluttered. "Is
she all right?"

Her dad frowned. "I honestly don't
know, Molly. Mrs Hunter said that Star's
stopped eating, which is very worrying.
I'm keeping Star here for the moment to
do some tests and try to work out what's
wrong."

"Can I come and see her?" Molly
asked eagerly.

Her dad nodded. "Maybe you can cheer
her up a bit."

Molly smiled gratefully at him. She just
hoped that when she saw Star she'd be
able to talk to her properly this time.

After lunch Molly and her dad walked back across the yard to the surgery.

"Do you think Star might be really sick, Dad?" Molly asked quietly. She knew that sometimes her dad just couldn't help. Everyone at the surgery hated it when that happened.

Molly's dad shook his head. "I don't think so, at the moment. I can't see anything wrong with her."

"Can I go and keep her company?" Molly's voice was hopeful.

"Yes, I've got quite a few cases coming

in this afternoon. Just be gentle, won't you? She's such a shy little dog." Her dad grinned and put an arm round her as they opened the surgery door. "I don't need to tell you that, do I, Molly? Probably you'll have Star all sorted out by the time I get through my appointments."

Molly smiled back. Of course her dad was joking, but she was so hoping that actually he was right. . .

Molly quietly opened the door to the animal ward. It was empty apart from the large run at the end, where Star was curled up on a comfy cushion. She was facing the wall, and she didn't even bother to turn round when Molly came in. Molly opened the run, and knelt by the door.

"Hey, Star," she murmured, trying not to scare the little dog.

Star peered over her shoulder wearily,
and politely sniffed Molly's fingers.

Molly shivered. She had to find out
what was wrong. She reached into the
cage and lifted the puppy out. At last Star
looked up, and a mist seemed to clear
away from her eyes.

"It's you!" she breathed. "I remember
you!" She jumped up and stood with her

front paws on Molly's chest, looking into her face. "You're magical too, I could feel it. You wanted to help me!"

Molly nodded slowly. The worry about Star was seeping away from her mind now, and she could feel the excitement bubbling up inside her. Star was talking to her!

Molly shook herself. That wasn't what was important right now. "What's wrong, Star? Have you lost your owner? Or is it that you don't like Mrs Hunter? She's really nice, you know."

"No, no!" Star shook her head so that her long ears flapped prettily. "She's lovely. She misses her old dog, I can tell, but I know I'll be happy there. I could make her happy too, I know we could, if only. . ." She sighed, and looked miserably at Molly.

"She only took me," Star whispered, and Molly could feel that it hurt her to talk about it. "We tried to tell her, Stella and I, but she couldn't hear us. We *have* to be together. We're twins, but it's more than that. We're wish puppies. We belong together − when Stella and I are together, we can do anything," she added proudly. "We can grant you any wish you like!"

Molly laughed delightedly. "I knew it! I knew there was something special about you. Magic twin puppies, that's so amazing! Can you really grant wishes? If I wished for something now, would it really come true?"

Star looked thoughtfully at Molly, with her head on one side and her lip curling a little in a shy dog smile. "What is your absolute favourite thing to eat?" she asked.

"What would you like best right this minute?"

Molly licked her lips just thinking about it. "Mint choc-chip ice cream! With chocolate sauce, like my mum makes sometimes."

Star hopped off Molly's knee and sat in front of her in a perfect china dog pose. She closed her eyes, and went very still.

There was a sudden shimmer of purple sparkles all around them and a pretty pink bowl dropped into Molly's hands. Molly gasped excitedly and then gulped.

It wasn't ice cream. The bowl was full of broccoli, Molly's worst ever food, that she was always arguing with Mum over. Molly was disappointed for a second, but then the funny side of it struck her. Magic broccoli! She giggled.

Star was gazing anxiously into the bowl. "That isn't right, is it?" she asked slowly.

"No. . . But it's a beautiful bowl," Molly added quickly, not wanting to upset her.

Star's ears drooped. "I should have been able to do that," she murmured worriedly. "I knew it. I could feel it. It's fading. I'm losing my magic, Molly!"

"What do you mean?" Molly asked in horror. She picked Star up and cuddled her close, feeling the little dog's heart banging against her ribs.

"It's because I'm not with Stella," Star muttered miserably into Molly's jumper. "We usually do magic together, but a little thing like a bowl of ice cream, I shouldn't need Stella for that. The magic is going. Maybe it's gone already!" Her voice was shaking.

"No, no, it can't be," Molly told her, hoping she was right. "If it had gone, nothing would have happened when you tried to make the ice cream. I know the magic didn't work the way it was supposed to, but even broccoli coming out of nowhere is pretty special, you know."

"Perhaps," Star murmured. "But what

can I do? The longer Stella and I are apart, the weaker we'll get. Oh, Molly, I have to find her!"

"*We* have to find her," Molly said firmly. "I'll help." She thought back to Star's first visit to the surgery. "Mrs Hunter said she got you from a farm not far from here. Do you know where it is?"

Star shook her head, but already she was looking more hopeful. Molly guessed that Star really needed another person to talk to – she just wasn't used to being without Stella. "I was in a box, and I was crying for Stella, so I wasn't really thinking. But you're right, it can't have been far. Oh, Molly, now you're here, I know we can find her! I knew you were special from the first time you picked me up!"

Molly smiled at her, and stroked her fluffy ears. "I'm sure we can too. There are lots of farms round here, but I shouldn't think many of them breed dogs. We should be able to work out which one it is, no problem." *But then what are we going to do?* Molly suddenly wondered. *I can't kidnap a puppy!*

Chapter Three

A Midnight Trip

"How's it going, Molly?" Molly's dad put his head round the door, and Molly tried not to look guilty. She hadn't actually been doing anything wrong, but she didn't fancy explaining that Star could talk. She scooted the bowl of broccoli behind her with her foot.

"I think Star's just lonely," Molly told her dad.

"She definitely looks a bit happier

now." Molly's dad crouched down to look.
"I need to have a proper look at her, and
your mum says to tell you to go back
and do your homework, OK?"

Molly sighed. "OK." She gave Star one
last hug, and whispered in her ear, "Don't
worry, I'll be back, I promise."

Star rubbed her silky ears against
Molly's cheek, and then let Molly pass her
over to her dad. As Molly's dad carried
her back into the consulting room, Star
was staring over his shoulder at Molly

all the way. Molly could hear her secret
message, and see it in her eyes.

*Come back soon. We need you, Molly. We're
running out of time!*

Molly threw the broccoli away in the
kitchen bin. Then she carried the pink
bowl up to her room to admire while
she was doing her reading for school. She
couldn't concentrate though. All she could
think of was how to find Stella, and bring
her and Star back together.

Maybe she could look up dog-breeders
on the computer? Then she had a brilliant
idea. Dad's map! He had one marked
with all the farms in the area, in case he
got called out to see a sick animal. Molly
nipped quickly down and borrowed it
from the drawer in the kitchen.

Back in her room, she spread it out

on the bed. Wow, there were lots! But Molly knew some of the closer ones. None of them had dogs. And that one, Sweethill Farm, wasn't that where Sam from school lived? Sam's parents only had chickens. It took ages but at last Molly had a list of six farms – one of them had to be Star's old home. Molly went back to her homework, glancing

occasionally at the list, as though it might tell her something. She couldn't wait to show it to Star.

"Molly, will you come and play with me? You haven't played with me all day!" Kitty pleaded, running in and bouncing on the end of Molly's bed.

Molly smiled at her little sister. She looked a bit like Star, with big, begging brown eyes. "All right. What do you want to play?" Molly checked her watch quickly. When was she going to fit in going back to the surgery? It was nearly tea time, almost the end of surgery hours, and Mum and Dad wouldn't let her go over there when no one else was around. Perhaps she could nip back now? She'd been doing her reading for ages – or holding the book, at least. But Kitty was happily chattering on about the game they were going to play. She couldn't tell Kitty she wasn't going to play with her now.

But when was she going to go? She couldn't wait until tomorrow. What if Star's magic was running out this very minute? Molly had to tell her the names of the farms, to see if she remembered which was hers.

Actually, it would be better to be at the surgery when no one else was there, if only she was allowed. Then there wouldn't be anyone to walk in and catch her talking to Star. As Molly walked over to the meadow with Kitty, a daring plan formed in her mind, making her smile excitedly to herself, and shiver, just a little bit. The only time she could go to the surgery in secret was at night. The *middle* of the

night. She was
going to have to
go on a midnight
mission!

"Night, Molly.
Sleep well."
Molly's mum gave
her a hug, and Molly
snuggled under her duvet,
trying to look sleepy. She was sure she
wouldn't be able to get to sleep, but she
didn't want Mum to be suspicious.

As soon as her mum had shut the
door, Molly sat up, and grabbed her pink
kitten alarm clock from the bookshelf
by her bed. It meowed when the alarm
went off, which always made her laugh.
Molly set it for midnight, and tucked it
carefully under her pillow. She didn't want

to wake up anyone else in the house as well. Luckily Mum and Dad both went to sleep pretty early normally. Then she lay down again and sighed. Of course she wouldn't be able to sleep, she thought, yawning. And it was only eight o'clock. Four hours until she set off! What on earth was she going to do? Molly's eyes closed and then fluttered open, and she yawned. Waiting was so boring. . .

Molly jumped awake as the muffled mewing sounded in her ear. She shook her head sleepily, trying to work out what was going on. Oh! The alarm clock! Her special mission! Somehow it didn't seem so exciting in the middle of the night, when her bedroom was so very dark. And it was cold. Molly rummaged under her pillow and turned off the alarm, then sat up. She shivered, but threw back her duvet.

It was
dark for Star
too, down in
the surgery,
and she
was waiting
for Molly.

She'd been waiting ages, and she probably
thought Molly had given up.

Molly put on her dressing gown,
tucking the list into the pocket. She'd
grab her wellies to cross the yard when
she got downstairs. She'd hunted out her
torch before she went to bed, and now
she grabbed it and set off, trying not
to feel scared. It was only her house! It
wasn't as if she was going far − just across
the yard. In the dark.

Molly crept along the landing, trying
to remember which were the creaky

steps on the stairs. The farmhouse was old, and there were often strange noises in the night. Dad always said it was just the pipes. So hopefully Mum and Dad wouldn't get up if they heard anything.

Molly made it to the kitchen and breathed a sigh of relief. No one would hear her down here. Now, the keys. Mum kept them all on hooks on the wall. Yes! Here were the surgery keys, and the back door key to let herself out.

Funnily enough, it seemed lighter outside. The moon was shining brightly as Molly set off across the yard, unlike her torch which was worryingly feeble. It must be low on batteries. Molly shook it hopefully, but it made no difference. She couldn't stop to look for batteries now, she'd just have to manage.

Molly went on, and then realized she

was crunching across the gravel. She tried
to tiptoe but her wellies wouldn't bend
that way. She froze, and stared up at her
parents' window, but the light didn't go
on. Luckily it was a bit chilly for having

the windows open. Maybe the best thing
to do was just run and get to the surgery
as quickly as she could.

Molly flung herself across the yard and
arrived, heart thudding, at the back door
that went straight into the animal ward.
She fumbled for the right key, and at last
the door clicked open.

The room looked strange in the dark,
much bigger. Molly shone the torch
around, and eyes gleamed spookily out
of the darkness. Something was watching
her! Molly gasped, and then sighed out
a breath, her heartbeat slowing down
again. It was only the cats. Her dad had
mentioned that there were a couple of
cats in the ward that night, as he'd kept
them in that afternoon. He'd grumbled,
laughing, because he was going to have to
get up early to check on them.

Both the cats mewed hopefully at her, wondering if she was bringing them some food, and Molly went up to their pens. "Sorry, I haven't got anything for you," she murmured, reaching her fingers through and gently stroking them behind the ears, making them purr faintly. "I've just come to talk to Star."

Star was standing up in her pen, waiting anxiously for Molly. She looked like a little pale ghost in the torchlight. Was it Molly's imagination, or was Star herself fading away, not only her magic? Did wish puppies disappear, when they

couldn't grant wishes? That would be awful!

Molly let Star out of the pen and they curled up together in the old armchair that the veterinary nurses used when they had to feed baby animals.

"I'm so glad you came back," Star murmured, pressing her nose gratefully into Molly's neck. "I miss Stella so much, but you being here helps."

"I've been trying to think how we could find Stella," Molly told her. "I had an idea, look. I found my dad's map with all the farms round here on it. This is a list of farms that might be your one. Do you think you'd recognize the name of it?"

Star said, "Maybe. . ." but she sounded doubtful, and when Molly told her the names on the list, her eyes misted over with that strange, sad look again. "I don't remember any of them, Molly," she whispered.

"Don't worry." Molly tried to make her voice bright, but she knew it wasn't very convincing. "I'm sure it's one of those. We'll just have to try them all, somehow. . ."

But how? Molly didn't know but she wasn't going to give up. They *had* to find Stella. She hugged Star close, feeling the glittery, wonderful sense of magic running through the fur under her fingertips. "I don't suppose you could use your magic to search for Stella?" she asked hopefully.

"I did try, when I was first taken away," Star explained. "But I was so upset then, I couldn't find anything. Maybe if I try again now."

She sat up tensely on Molly's knee,

staring into the distance, clearly thinking hard about her sister. Her eyes sparkled for a second, and Molly took a hopeful breath. Was the magic about to work?

But then the magical light died away, and Star flopped sadly down on Molly's lap. "I can't make it work at all. I can hardly feel my magic, Molly. Without Stella, it's nearly all gone." Her voice was shaking, and her tiny body shook too.

Molly ran her hand down Star's silky

back. "It'll be all right. We'll find the farm," she promised her firmly. "I'll go back home and look on the computer now. If I search for those farms, one of them might have a website about breeding spaniels. We'll find her, Star. We really will."

Chapter Four

The Wishing Spell

Molly scurried carefully across the gravel again. She was planning to use the computer in the study and search the internet to see if one of those six farms was advertising King Charles spaniel puppies. Surely there wouldn't be more than one? She really hoped they did have a website, or a mention somewhere. They did lots of research on the computers at school, so she was pretty sure she could find it. Oh, if only Star had been able to use her magic even a little, just to give her some clues. But she couldn't do magic without her twin to help. She needed someone to join with. . .

Molly stopped suddenly in the middle of the yard, putting her hand up to the locket round her neck, the little cat face that Sparkle and the witch had given her. It had one of Sparkle's whiskers in it, so Molly could call him for help. She could feel the locket glowing in her fingers as a wonderful idea came to her. Star needed someone to join with, but did it have to be Stella? Maybe she should call Sparkle now? Perhaps he could join with Star, and help her use her magic?

Molly could feel the power of the locket in her hand. She thought about that wonderful, scary afternoon, when she'd taken Sparkle home. The witch had said Molly had a true gift for helping animals. Her magic wasn't only to talk to them, she could *do* things too. Molly and Sparkle had made a magic dust together – Molly really had helped him, even though she wasn't sure how. She could do things. . .

Maybe she didn't need to call Sparkle. Maybe there was a way that Star could use Molly's own magic to help her find Stella?

Molly was so excited that she forgot about being careful. She just ran back, waving her torch wildly. And she was so eager to find Star again that she didn't realize her torch batteries had finally given up. She was bathed in a silvery light as she tried to unlock the door with trembling fingers. At last she flung it open and raced back into the surgery. The two cats hissed with surprise as she burst in, and Star jumped up at the wire of her pen.

"Molly!" she barked. "You're shining!"

Molly looked down at her hands in surprise. Star was right. There was a silvery glow all round her, gleaming softly from her skin. Wow! That had never happened before. She turned her hands over, wiggling her fingers. It was still there!

Star scrabbled eagerly at the door of

her pen. She suddenly seemed more alive
than Molly had ever seen her, her tail
wagging with excitement. "Let me out!
Molly, quickly, please!"

Molly undid the latch. "What's happening,
Star? Did you do this? Is your magic
coming back after all?" she asked hopefully.

"No, this must be your power, Molly!
But that light, it's just like what happens
when Stella and I do magic – except our
light is pink. Don't you see what that
means? Maybe you and I could do magic
together to find Stella!"

Molly laughed delightedly. "But that's what I was coming back to say! I thought of it just now. I remembered that the witch told me I should use my power to help. I thought I might be able to take Stella's place, just this once."

Star nodded seriously. "I'm sure we can."

"What do we have to do?" Molly demanded, her voice eager.

Star sniffed the air thoughtfully. "We should go outside. We need to call to Stella, and we can't be shut in for that. Where's a good place, Molly?" She looked up at Molly, her deep, dark eyes shining with hope and love. It was love for Stella, but for Molly too, and it made Molly feel so special, knowing that Star trusted her.

I can't let them down! she told herself fiercely. *We have to do this — Star looks so much better already, just thinking that we might find Stella. She'd almost given up before.*

"The orchard?" Molly suggested. "It's beautiful there. Would that help?"

Star nodded. "If it's a special place for you, then it will be good for doing magic. Let's go, Molly!" She was dancing and jumping round Molly's legs, looking more like a puppy than Molly had ever seen her.

The silver glow lit their way as they opened the orchard gate. Star ran ahead, bouncing through the long grass, her ears flapping wildly. The moonlight was shining on the last of the apples, the ones at the tops of the trees that were too high to reach.

Star looked round at Molly. "This is the place," she said. "Molly, will you pick me up? We should be touching for the magic to work."

Molly scooped Star up in her arms,
and together they stared into the sky.
Molly felt Star's magic shimmering into
her own, and the silver light around
them became tinged with pink. The
warm glow of the magic seemed to
run through her body, and she shivered

delightedly and buried her face in Star's silky fur.

"Ohhh, wonderful," Star murmured. "It's like I haven't been able to breathe, and now I can. Now wish, Molly! Wish for Stella to come back to us!"

Molly nodded, and she whispered to the sky, "I'm wishing! I'm wishing!"

Star made a little whining noise. "Stella, can you hear us? We're wishing for you! Please come and find us. . . I need you. . ."

Molly sighed. How would they know if it was working? Had her power helped Star to make the wish come true?

All at once a cloud of silver stars rushed into the sky,

sparkling and shimmering, and carrying the wish with them.

Molly gasped with delight.

"That was it," Star said proudly.

"Oh! Does that mean it's worked?" Molly asked hopefully.

Star stared up at the stars glittering above them, the star-shine reflected in her dark eyes. "I hope so, Molly. I've never made a wish for myself before, but this is the most important wish of all. I hope it comes true. . ."

The wish stars flickered upwards until Molly and Star couldn't tell them apart from the real stars any more. Then the two of them sank down on to the grass, worn out with the effort of wishing.

They had done everything they could. Now they just had to wait.

Chapter Five

Star and Stella

Molly shivered and hugged Star tight. "It's getting cold," she whispered. "We should go back."

Star gave a reluctant whine, looking sadly up at Molly. Her eyes still shimmered with the silver wish-light, but she looked small and lonely. Molly stared at the tiny dog in her arms. Molly couldn't leave her to sleep on her own in that little pen, even though it did have a warm cushion, and chew toys.

"I know, but we can't stay out here all night. I wish we could, but we'll freeze." Molly stroked Star's ears gently. "I won't put you back in your pen," she muttered. "You're coming back to the house with me, Star." Molly didn't know what would happen in the morning, when Mum found Star in her room. She would get into trouble, but all of a sudden she was too tired to care.

She stood up, holding Star in her arms, and trudged slowly to the gate, and across the yard. At the back door, Molly paused, and they gazed up into the sky. Was it her imagination, or were there still a few wish sparkles floating there? Was it going to work? It just had to! "*Please. . .*" Molly murmured, not quite sure who she was talking to.

They crept up the stairs, a faint silver

light still glowing around them and
lighting their way. Star looked around
interestedly as they sneaked up into
Molly's room. "This is nice," she said
sleepily, curling into a small shining ball on
Molly's duvet. Molly started to answer her,
but then realized that the puppy was fast
asleep. Obviously wishing was hard work!

Molly hung up her dressing gown, yawning hugely. Seeing Star all snuggled up like that made her feel so sleepy too. She crawled carefully under the duvet, trying not wake up Star, who'd chosen a place right in the middle of the bed. Molly ended up with her nose pressed against the wall, but she didn't mind. Star's peaceful breathing shushed in her ears, and she drifted off to sleep.

"Hey," Molly murmured sleepily. She was having a strange dream. Somebody was licking her – it felt like a dog. Whoever it was, they were very determined about it. They kept going, even when she tried to wriggle away. Eventually Molly realized that she wasn't dreaming. There really *was* a dog very thoroughly licking her ear. Star! Molly sat bolt

upright, suddenly remembering her
adventures of the night before.

"At last! I've been trying to wake you for ages!" Star was bouncing up and down on the bed beside her, her ears flapping joyfully.

Molly stared at her, slowly taking in how different she looked. Star's eyes were shining with happiness. She'd lost the strange, ghostly look that had made it look as though she was only half there. Her coat was thick and glossy, her brown patches shining as though she'd been polished. Altogether she looked like a different dog from the sad, quiet little creature of yesterday.

"Come on!" Star barked happily. "Ooops, sorry, Molly!" She stuck her head under the duvet, giggling. Then she wriggled further down, enjoying her game, and little pink sparkles trickled out from under the edges of the duvet.

It looked like Star's power was well and truly back.

Even though she was worried about Mum or Dad hearing, Molly couldn't help laughing too. Star's happiness was filling the room.

Star's black nose peeped out from under the duvet. "Come on!" she said again, whispering this time. "Stella's near, I can feel her! Come *on*, Molly!"

Molly jumped out of bed. "She's here already? Oh, Star, that's wonderful!" Molly scrambled into jeans and a jumper, and they raced downstairs. Molly hadn't bothered to look at her clock in the rush, but she was sure it was still quite early. It didn't feel like she'd had very much sleep, but she was too excited to feel tired.

Star was jumping and scrabbling eagerly

at the back door. "She's here, Molly, she's here! Let me out!"

Molly unlocked the door, and swung it open, looking anxiously out into the yard.

Sitting on the back step was a beautiful little dog, staring up at her with hopeful eyes. Molly gasped. She was the image of Star! The same gorgeous fluffy ears; big, dark eyes, and cute snub nose. Even the identical joyful expression as the two puppies flung themselves at each other with delighted little whines.

"It worked! Oh, Star, it worked!" Molly murmured, watching the two puppies rubbing their heads together lovingly. She crouched down beside them. "I can't believe how alike you look. Even the spots on your backs are the same."

Stella looked up at her. "They're not quite the same, you know," she said, her voice a softer version of Star's, as though perhaps she wasn't as used to talking to people. "Look. . ." And she and Star sat down together with their backs turned to Molly, each peering over their shoulder and giving her dog-smiles, their pink tongues showing.

"Oh! Yes, I can see now. They're opposites, aren't they? Like you're one dog looking in a mirror. It's so pretty, it's almost as though the spots join up." Molly turned her head to one side. "They do! It's a heart shape, a perfect heart!"

The dogs nodded at her. "That's why we're wish puppies, Molly," Star explained.

"We're *very* rare," Stella added.

"And now we're together, we can grant wishes again." Star touched noses joyfully with Stella.

"How did you do it, Star?" Stella asked. "I'd worn myself out wishing for you to come back, but it never worked. Without you I just couldn't make the wishes happen. I'd given up. I was sure I wouldn't ever be a magic dog again, and then last night I felt a wish sparkling all over me. It woke me up and I felt so happy. Then suddenly I was outside my run, and there was a trail of silver stars glittering in the grass. I followed them, they smelled delicious, like the best dog biscuits. And they led me here."

"It was Molly," Star said, staring up at her gratefully. "She wanted to help, but we couldn't work out how. Then I saw her glowing, like we do when we make wishes, and I thought perhaps she could be a wish-girl, to get you back for me. And it worked!"

"I've never heard of a wish-girl." Stella looked at Molly admiringly. "You know what this means, don't you, Star?" she told her twin.

Star nodded. "Definitely."

The pair of them gazed up at Molly, and she stepped back worriedly. "What is it?"

"You've saved us, Molly. You've brought us back together, so now we will give you a wish. A very special wish, to say thank you. What do you want most of all?" Star and Stella had tiny pink sparkles twinkling over their fur already, and Molly was pretty sure that whatever she wished for, she would get. No magic broccoli this time. But what should she ask for? A wish! It was so special, so important. She mustn't waste it.

All at once, Molly knew. It was what she had wanted for so long. She closed her eyes, ready to speak the words aloud—

But then she had a sudden thought. She opened her eyes again, looking down worriedly at the puppies. *What was going to happen to them now?* Mrs Hunter had only wanted one dog. Would she take Stella as well? And how was Molly going to explain that Star's twin had suddenly appeared? Dad wasn't going to believe it, whatever she said.

Molly sighed. She knew what her wish had to be. She closed her eyes again.

"I wish that Star and Stella find a home together," she said firmly. "And that they make Mrs Hunter happy." She smiled as she said that last bit. Even though it was disappointing not to use the wish for herself, she could just imagine Star and Stella dragging Mrs Hunter all over the town, and the old lady laughing.

She opened her eyes again, and sat down on the step with a bump. Star and Stella were surrounded by a beautiful pink

and purple cloud, and the heart shape
on their backs seemed to glow. Then the
colours faded, and the wish puppies shook
themselves.

"Oh, Molly!" Star said, surprised. "That was supposed to be a wish for you!"

"It was for me!" Molly smiled at her. "I'd be ever so worried about you, wouldn't I, if I hadn't done it? Besides, maybe that wish will stop Dad finding out I went into the surgery in the middle of the night!" she added. "He'd be really cross!"

"She deserves another wish, since she used her wish for us," Stella said firmly. "I could do another, Star, couldn't you? I can tell you had something else you wanted, Molly, I could see it in your eyes."

"Of course I could!" Star said indignantly. "Molly has a loving heart. We should definitely give her another wish."

The two puppies stared up at her expectantly, and Molly smiled. "I'm so glad you're going to find a home," she whispered to them. "I know you'll be happy. But my wish is that one day, I don't mind when, really, as long as it isn't too long. . . One day, please could I have a pet of my own?"

Star and Stella looked at each other and nodded.

"Oh yes!" Star breathed. "It's a good wish!"

"A special wish!" Stella agreed, and once again the pink and purple swirling mist rippled around them, and this time Molly felt silvery threads wrapping round her too. There was a wonderful floating feeling as the mist swept round her, shimmering in and out and through – and then it was gone, leaving just a sense of happiness.

"It worked, didn't it?" Molly asked, as

the puppies blinked sleepily at her.

"Oh yes. . ." Star yawned. "Sorry, Molly,

I'm tired. Two wishes at once is ever such a lot. We even had to borrow some of your magic again to make sure." She climbed into Molly's lap, and curled up snugly. "Come on, Stella," she murmured, and the second wish puppy followed her sister, nudging her over to make room.

"You need a bigger lap," she told Molly, as she fell asleep.

Molly smiled down at them, one ball of brown and gold fur, and she leaned against the door frame and closed her eyes too, dreaming of her own pet, at last. . .